Favorite Fairy
Peter Pan

Retold by Rochelle Larkin   Illustrated by Jesse Zerner

CREATIVE CHILD PRESS
is a registered trademark of Playmore Inc.,
Publishers and Waldman Publishing Corp., New York, N.Y.

Once upon a time a girl named Wendy Darling lived with her brothers, John and Michael, and their parents in London.

But one night, when their parents were out to dinner and their dog Nana had been tied up in the yard for barking, two curious visitors came into the Darling family's house.

One was a boy named Peter Pan, who was looking for his shadow. The other was his friend Tinker Bell, a mischievous little fairy who often played tricks on everyone.

Wendy was startled when she saw this strange boy in her room, but Peter said not to be afraid. He told her about Never Never Land, where he lived.

Peter said that he would take them all to Never Never Land. He taught them how to fly.

There was every sort of adventure to be had in Never Never Land. There were pirates and Indians. The pirates, headed by Captain Hook, were very bad, but Tiger Lily and the Indians were Peter's friends.

Peter explained about the crocodile who had swallowed a big ticking alarm clock, so they could always tell when it was around.

Wendy was welcomed by the lost boys, who liked to think she was their mother. Wendy took care of them, fixing their food and mending their clothes.

John and Michael tried to be adventurous, but the thought of pirates worried them.

The pirate chief, Captain Hook, was after the lost boys, especially Peter, since it was because of Peter that he had a hook for a hand.

When Wendy and the others arrived, the lost boys were looking for Peter, the pirates were looking for the boys, the Indians were looking for the pirates, and the wild animals were looking for the Indians. Never Never Land was on the move.

Peter and the lost boys lived underground for safety's sake.
They showed the Darlings how to get in and out through the
hollowed-out tree trunks. They thought it was great fun,
sliding up and down.

Everything went well, but at last it was time for the Darlings to go back home, taking the lost boys with them.

Peter refused to leave Never Never Land. He didn't ever want to grow up. But he asked Tiger Lily to have the Indians lead the others through the island, and Tinker Bell to guide them across the sea.

But at the very moment they were ready, the pirates attacked the Indians.

The Darling children and the lost boys flew back to London. Only Peter stayed. Mr. and Mrs. Darling were thrilled to have their own children back and adopted all the others.

When Wendy had
a daughter of her own, Peter took little Jane with
him to Never Never Land to do all the things
Wendy had done.

Even after all the children grew up, they always remembered
Peter Pan.